Copyright 2020 RovenLit
All Rights Reserved.
No part of this book may be reproduced or transmitted
by any form or by any means, electronic or mechanical,
including photocopy, recording, or any information storage
or retrieval system, without prior written consent from the author.

Printed in the United States of America
First Printing, 2020
ISBN: 978-1-7366915-7-1 paperback

Written by Dominga Santos
Illustrated by sisters Sarah and Ari Roven

I dedicate this book to my son, Pascual Umansky
-D.S.

Dedicated to our little amorcitos A, C, & E2
We love you beyond words
-A.S.

Thank you to our amigas Mireya Calderon, Iona Levin,
Nomi Laio, and Raymonde Barishman for helping
to write this book. Without your love, support,
and influence over the years
this book would not exist.
-A&S

Thank you to my partner in crime Sergio Umansky Brener
and my awesome family and friends.
I love you,
-D.S.

In the great big room
There was a manta on the sofá
And a vase of beautiful flores
And a picture on the wall of —

Mis amores

And there were three bears,
pasando el rato,
on hand-painted wood chairs

And there were two maracas
And a plate of tortilla
And on the shelf a game of Lotería

And tidying up the house was Abuelita
Wearing a fancy golden cadenita

And in the dining room was Abuelito
Enjoying desert, pastelito
Sitting with our perro named Pepito

Goodnight vase of beautiful flores

Goodnight picture of mis amores

Goodnight bears
Goodnight hand-painted chairs

Goodnight maracas

Goodnight tortilla

Goodnight game of Lotería

Goodnight Abuelita

Goodnight fancy gold cadenita

Goodnight Abuelito

Goodnight yummy pastelito

And goodnight my perro,
our sweet Pepito

Goodnight my sweet amorcitos
Que sueñes con los angelitos
Te quiero forever
Life is much better when we're together

Glossary

For all the non-Spanish speakers out there, we warmly welcome you. To enjoy the book as much as possible follow the glossary below.

Mis Amores: Literally translates in Spanish to 'my loves.' A term of endearment typically said to children.

Manta: Blanket in Spanish

Florero Bonito: Beautiful vase

Pasando El Rato: Translates to 'hanging out' in Spanish. The three bears are 'hanging out' on three Spanish style chairs.

Maracas: Maracas originated from the indigenous tribes of Latin America. They are musical instruments that are similar in appearance to baby rattles in the United States. However, in Latin countries maracas are not just for children- they are for everyone as they are a celebratory Spanish product. Many Latin musicians use maracas still today!

Tortilla: Tortillas are a delicious flat bread originating in Mexico form Aztec origin. Over the years they have changed in many ways so they look and taste different in every Latin country. In fact, in Mexico tortillas are flat but in Spain tortillas are a completely different food made with potatoes and eggs. Check the back of this book for a recipe to make your own yummy homemade Mexican flour tortillas!

Lotería: Loteria is a famous game in every Latin home. The game actually originated in Italy in the 1400s and was brought to Spain and Mexico in 1770. Over the decades it has become a tradition in Latin American homes. If you're able to try the game we know you will have a lot of fun!

Abuelita: 'Grandma' in Spanish

Cadenita: Necklace in Spanish. In this story it's a golden cadenita (a gold necklace).

Abuelito: 'Grandpa' in Spanish

Pastelito: This is the Spanish word for 'cake' or 'pastry.' Usually pastelito refers to a slice of cake or a small desssert

Perro: Dog in Spanish

Pepito: Pepito is a popular name in Spanish - cute for any male!

Mi amorcitos: translates in Spanish to 'my little love.' Spanish is a Latin language - 'amor' means love and 'cito' at the end of any noun makes it 'little.'

Que sueñes con los angelitos: 'Sweet dreams, sleep with the angels.' This is a common bedtime phrase in Spanish

Te quiero: 'I love you' in Spanish

Buenas Noches: Goodnight in Spanish

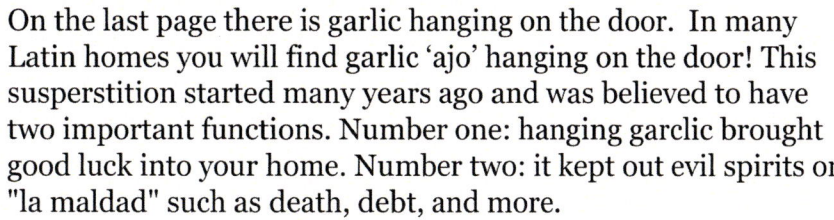

Did you notice?

If you noticed, this book has some funny things in Spanish culture.

On the last page there is garlic hanging on the door. In many Latin homes you will find garlic 'ajo' hanging on the door! This susperstition started many years ago and was believed to have two important functions. Number one: hanging garclic brought good luck into your home. Number two: it kept out evil spirits or "la maldad" such as death, debt, and more.

There is also a sign on the last page that says "L'HE URE DE LA SIESTE" as the grandfather and dog sleep on the sofa. In many Spanish countries people take a break mid-day called 'Siesta Time' there where they literally take a nap mid-day! Sounds lovely, right?! Siesta time is usually a few hours after lunch, like 2pm, and it originated as a way to make it through working late into the night in many Latin countries.

Also on the last page is a classic Mexican doll on the floor next to the little baby. These handmade dolls are also known as Rag dolls or 'María Dolls'. The dolls originated in Michoacán, Mexico and were initially created so that those who could not afford a porcelain doll could have their own doll, because they were made by community members. Many mother's continue to make these dolls handmade for their children today!

In the dining room there are chilli's hanging on the cabinet. What can we say? Latin's love their spicy chillis and hang them everywhere!

Last but not least, there is a Spanish fan on every fireplace.

Recipe time!

Abuelita's Homemade Tortillas

Ingredients

3 cups flour (white or whole wheat depending on preference)
1 teaspoon salt
1 teaspoon baking powder
1 cup warm water
⅓ cup olive oil or vegetable oil
parchment paper

Directions:

   First combine dry ingredients (flour, salt, and baking powder) in a bowl. Thoroughly mix dry ingredients together.
Make a well in the center of the dry ingredients and add the oil and water. Stir well all the ingredients and mix until the dough begins to form a shaggy ball. Knead the dough for 1-2 minutes until there are no lumps and the dough is a smooth round shape. Divide dough into 15 equal round balls. Flatten the dough balls with the palm of your hand and cover them with a clean kitchen towel for at least 15 minutes (you can and allow the balls of dough to rest as long as 2 hours before continuing).

   Heat a large pan over medium heat. With a roller, roll each ball of dough into a circle, about 7 inches in diameter. When the pan is hot, place one dough circle into the pan and allow it to cook for 1 minute (or until the bottom surface has a few brown spots and the uncooked surface is bubbling a little bit). Flip the tortilla to the other side and cook for 15-20 seconds. The tortillas should be soft but have a few small brown spots on the surface. If the tortillas are browning too fast, reduce the heat. Place the hot finished tortilla on a plate followed by a piece of parchment paper. The parchment paper must be in between each fresh hot tortilla or they will stick to one another.

And that's it, you've made you're first homemade tortilla!
Enjoy!

The End
&
Buenas Noches

Made in United States
Orlando, FL
16 July 2024